Wesley
WENDELL

IN THE GARDEN

SHEP IRELAND

A WESLEY AND WENDELL BOOK

The C.R. Gibson Company, Norwalk, Connecticut 06856

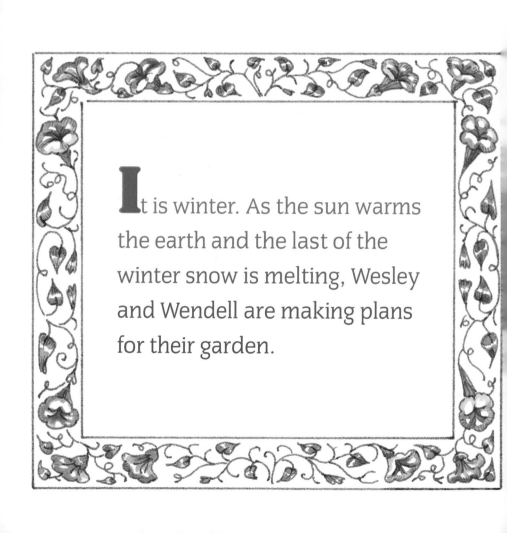

It is winter. As the sun warms the earth and the last of the winter snow is melting, Wesley and Wendell are making plans for their garden.

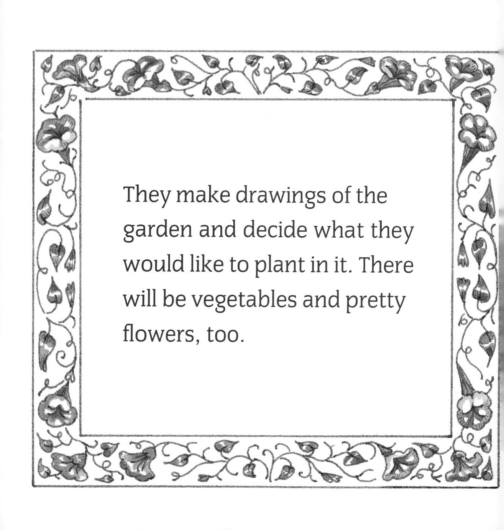

They make drawings of the garden and decide what they would like to plant in it. There will be vegetables and pretty flowers, too.

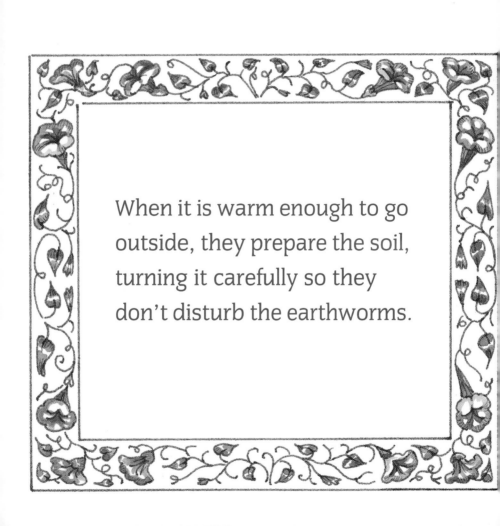

When it is warm enough to go outside, they prepare the soil, turning it carefully so they don't disturb the earthworms.

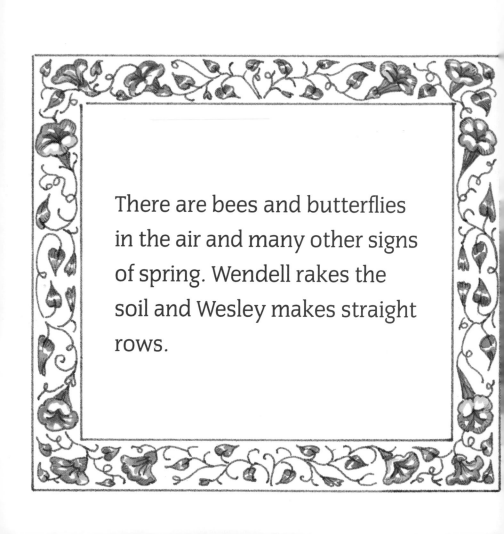

There are bees and butterflies in the air and many other signs of spring. Wendell rakes the soil and Wesley makes straight rows.

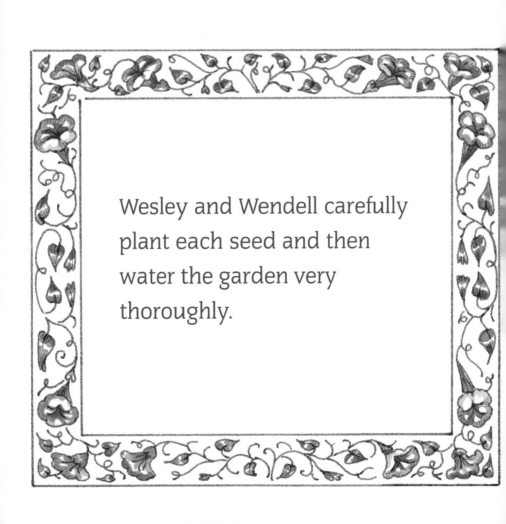

Wesley and Wendell carefully plant each seed and then water the garden very thoroughly.

They put up a wire fence
around their garden to protect
it.

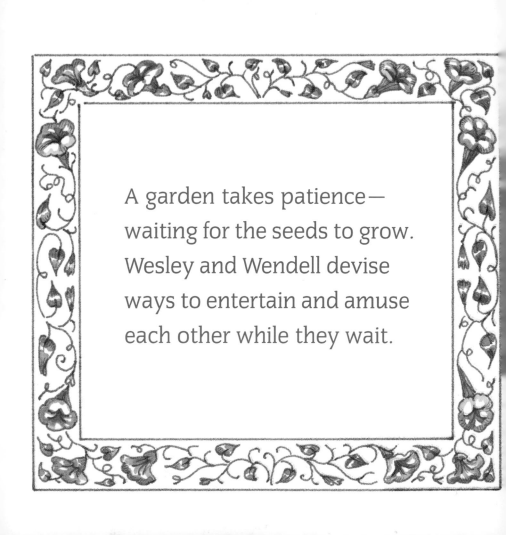

A garden takes patience—
waiting for the seeds to grow.
Wesley and Wendell devise
ways to entertain and amuse
each other while they wait.

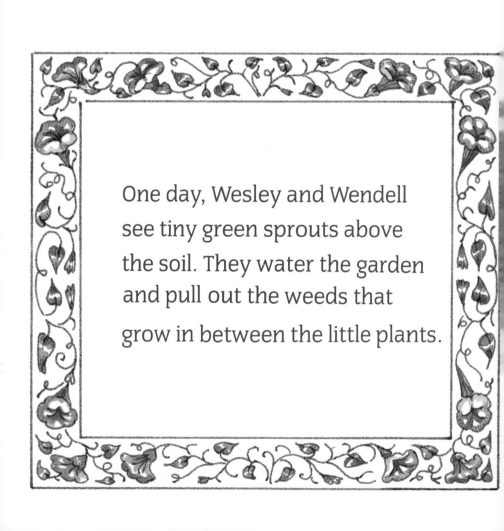

One day, Wesley and Wendell see tiny green sprouts above the soil. They water the garden and pull out the weeds that grow in between the little plants.

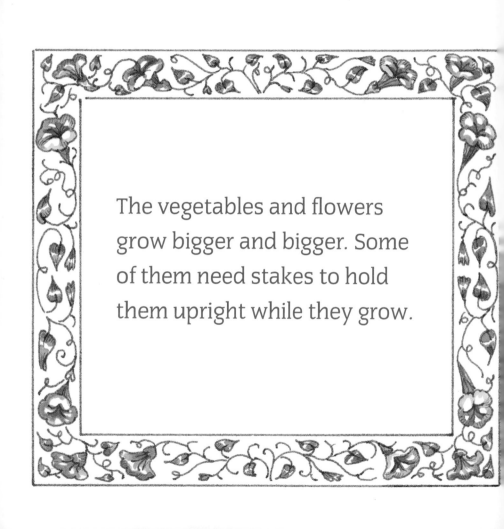

The vegetables and flowers grow bigger and bigger. Some of them need stakes to hold them upright while they grow.

Wesley and Wendell make a scarecrow to keep birds away from the garden.

On rainy days they can't work
in the garden, so Wesley and
Wendell repair the roadside
stand where they will sell
some of their crops.

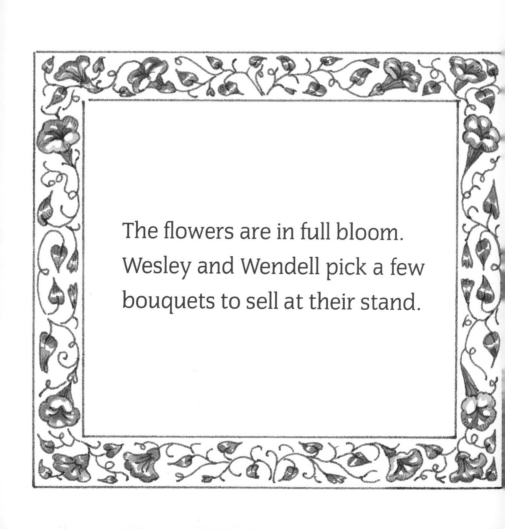

The flowers are in full bloom. Wesley and Wendell pick a few bouquets to sell at their stand.

There is one sure way to be sure that the vegetables are ready to harvest. Yum!

Friends and neighbors come
to buy their wonderful vegetables
and flowers. This money will
buy new seeds and tools for
next year.

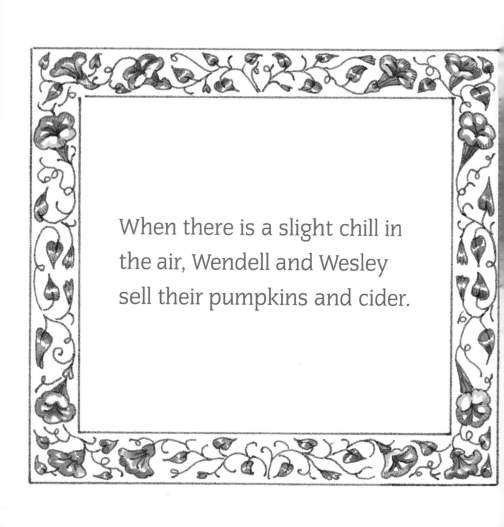

When there is a slight chill in the air, Wendell and Wesley sell their pumpkins and cider.

Now it is fall and the garden
must be trimmed back
and covered with salt hay
and leaves to protect it from
the cold.

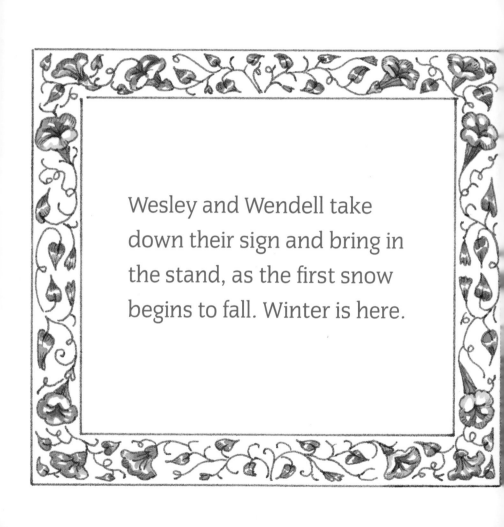

Wesley and Wendell take down their sign and bring in the stand, as the first snow begins to fall. Winter is here.

What a wonderful year it has been!